HOPELESS

HADES' PET HELLHOUND!

STELLA TARAKSON

Sweet Cherry

First published in the UK by Sweet Cherry Publishing Limited, 2020
Unit 36, Vulcan House, Vulcan Road,
Leicester, LE5 3EF,
United Kingdom

Sweet Cherry Europe (Europe address)
Nauschgasse 4/3/2 POB 1017
Vienna, WI 1220, Austria

10 9

ISBN: 978-1-78226-353-1

Illustrations by Nick Roberts

www.sweetcherrypublishing.com

Printed and bound in India

For everyone at Sweet Cherry,

for making this possible

Tim Baker couldn't believe what was happening. He was flying – hurtling through time and space – with Leo the bully, of all people.

Leo had figured out Tim's secret. Not all of it, but enough to make him determined to ferret out the rest. First he'd overheard Tim talking to the old Greek vase. Then, while Leo watched, a golden mist had appeared, completely covering Tim and the vase. When the mist lifted, both had vanished.

Tim had hoped that Leo would forget what he'd seen, or at least think that he'd imagined it. No such luck. Like a pit bull with a trouser leg, Leo hadn't let go. Realising that Tim had been ordering the vase to take him somewhere, Leo had finally blustered his way into Tim's home, grabbed the vase, and ordered it to take him wherever it took Tim. Now they were both headed for Ancient Greece.

The wind roared in Tim's ears as they flew through the air. He stole a glance at Leo's face. The boy's eyes were wide as he tried to see through the golden mist surrounding them. Tim had to admire his

courage. The first time he'd travelled with
the vase, Tim had been so scared that he
kept his eyes clamped shut.

'What's happening?' Leo shouted.

'You'll see.'

Tim's adventures had begun when
he accidentally broke the old Greek
vase, and Hercules had emerged from
the pieces. The hero had been trapped

for thousands of years by the wicked goddess Hera, and quickly became firm friends with Tim. It was Hercules' encouragement that had finally helped Tim to stand up to Leo – something Tim would always be grateful for.

Gone were the days when Tim felt awkward and uncertain. In Ancient Greece especially, he was a better, stronger person. Nobody called him Cinderella, the nickname Leo had invented to tease him about housework. People in the past thought Tim was brave and clever. He'd been called a hero by the goddess Athena!

'See what? You'd better tell me, Cinderella.'

Tim pressed his lips together. As happy as he always was to see his Ancient Greek friends, how could he unleash Leo on them?

When Hercules had escaped the vase into the modern world, he'd been invisible to everyone except Tim. The hero had even knocked Leo down once, much to the angry boy's confusion. But Hercules wasn't invisible anymore. Leo would put two and two together and get five: five fingers, in a fist, straight into Tim's face. Then Hercules would seek revenge, Zoe would get involved, and all hell would break loose. Tim shuddered.

Leo didn't know it, but the vase had to obey his every command. The spell "He who holds me commands me" was written on it in Ancient Greek. By grabbing the vase, Leo had put himself in control – and Tim was powerless to stop him.

Or was he? He was holding the vase, too …

Maybe he could reverse Leo's order.

'Oh vase,' Tim said, ignoring Leo's glare, 'take us back home.'

Never before had Tim changed instructions mid-flight. The vase paused. It wobbled, as if uncertain what to do.

'Hey, no!' Leo shouted. 'Take us where Tim goes.' The vase started moving forwards again.

'I said take us home!' The vase started to reverse.

'FORWARDS!'

shouted Leo, at the exact same moment
that Tim shouted

'BACKWARDS!'

The vase went neither backwards
nor forwards. It shuddered to a halt. It
hovered in the air for a moment. Then it
plunged straight down.

Tim clung desperately to the vase as it plummeted. This had never happened before! They must have confused it by giving conflicting instructions. Like an angry horse, the vase was trying to shake them off.

'Dude!' Leo shouted. 'What have you done?'

'It's not my fault!' Tim cried.

'Is too! I'm gonna get you for this.'

If the ground didn't get them first, Tim thought grimly. What was the point of arguing? Right now it didn't matter whose fault it was.

'Oh vase,' Tim ordered, forcing himself to stay calm. 'Take us home.'

'No way! Oi vase, take us where you take Tim.'

The vase dropped even faster.

'Are you mad?' Tim squeaked. 'We're confusing it. We have to tell it the same thing.'

'You just don't want me to know where you go!' Leo shouted over the sound of the rushing wind.

 'VASE, TAKE US

HOME. NOW!'

A look of anger crossed Leo's face
and Tim felt a stab of fear. What if the
other boy tried to push him off? Then
Leo could make the vase take him to
Ancient Greece alone. He'd meet Zoe
and Hercules and Agatha. He might pick
a fight with them. Or worse, he might
become friends with them! He might take
Tim's place, and his friends would forget
all about him.

Tim shuddered. Best not to think about
it. He held on to the slippery handle as
if his life depended on it. Which it did.
Maybe, for safety's sake, he should let Leo
have his way. The vase would land at Zoe's
house. Then, once Tim had a chance to

think, he could work out what to do.

'You win,' Tim said. 'Vase, take us to Zoe's house.'

But the vase continued to fall.

'I said take us to Zoe's!' Tim squeaked in panic.

'PLEASE!'

It didn't work. They had lost control. As if sulking, the vase accelerated. Tim closed his eyes. Hopefully it would slow down and give them a soft landing, at least. Goodness knows where – and when – they'd end up.

'Hey, little buddy. What are you doing up here?'

Tim's eyes snapped open. The messenger god Hermes hovered beside

him, the wings on his cap flapping
vigorously. The god's lips curled into a
crooked grin as he matched his descent to
the vase's.

'Help!' Tim cried. 'The vase has gone
mad!'

'Who's your friend?' Hermes nodded

at Leo, whose eyes bulged at the sight of the flying god.

'I'll explain later,' Tim said. 'Hurry!'

Hermes swiftly snatched one of Tim's hands with his right hand, and one of Leo's with his left. They immediately stopped falling. 'Keep hold of the vase,' Hermes warned. 'Don't want to break it again, do we?'

Tim felt weak with relief. He never knew what to make of Hermes. Although the young god served Hera, sometimes he seemed to be on Tim's side. And now he'd saved his life! It was very confusing.

With a nod and a wink, Hermes deposited them on Zoe's doorstep. 'Catch ya later,' he said, before flapping away.

Tim couldn't help noticing that the god's flight wasn't as smooth as usual. It was lopsided, like a sprinter running with a sprained ankle. Had he sprained one of his wings?

Tim shook himself. He didn't have time to worry about Hermes' wings now. He had bigger problems.

Tim tugged at the vase and Leo surrendered it without a struggle. He was too busy gaping at the row of simple mud-brick buildings, which were so unlike anything at home.

'Where did you bring us, Cinderella? It isn't even London!'

'We're not in Kansas anymore, Toto,' Tim replied, quoting from *The Wizard of Oz*.

'Then where on earth are we? Hey! I bet this isn't even Earth!' Leo took a menacing step towards Tim. 'This is another planet, isn't it? That flying guy's an alien.'

'We're not–'

'Gimme that vase. I'm going home before they start experimenting on me.'

Tim tucked the vase behind his back. 'Of course this is Earth, dummy.'

'Oh yeah? Then explain the flying guy.'

Tim clenched his fists. 'I'm not explaining anything. I didn't ask you to come. Why couldn't you just mind your own business?'

'Who lives here?' Leo pointed at Zoe's house. 'Can they fly, too?'

'My friends. And no, they can't fly.'

'Friends? Since when do you have friends?' Leo snorted. 'Other than that prat Ajay.'

Tim didn't bother answering. He had no intention of sharing his Greek friends with someone who'd forced their way into his secret world.

'Look, this is what we're going to do.' Tim made his voice sound strong. 'We're going to take a handle each, and *I* will order the vase to take us home. You're going to forget all about this. If you don't, I'll set that flying guy on you.'

Leo snorted. 'Nice try, Cinderella. If *you* don't want me here, then I'm staying. You're just scared that your friends will like me more than they like you.'

'Don't be ridiculous,' Tim said, even though that was exactly what he was thinking. 'What happens if I knock on that door right now?' Leo lifted his beefy fist to bang on Zoe's front door.

'Oh no you don't!' Tim threw himself at Leo and gripped his fist with both hands.

Grunting and cursing, the boys wrestled on the doorstep: Tim trying to pull Leo away from the house, while Leo kept hurling himself back towards it.

'Quiet,' Tim hissed. 'They'll hear us!'

'Well in that case ...' Leo took a deep breath and shouted,

'OI! OPEN UP!'

'Shut up!'

'Make me.'

Tim tried. Reaching over, he clamped his hand over the boy's mouth. But it was too late. Tim and Leo froze mid-tussle as the front door opened.

Tim and Leo barely had time to disentangle
before a small, dark-haired girl leapt
out onto the street. 'Tim!' Zoe shouted,
throwing her arms around his waist.

'YOU'RE BACK!'

Tim grinned. Having recently seen Zoe
as a lifeless statue, he was glad to see her
so excitable now. And since she insisted
that it hadn't been Hera's doing, Tim

still wondered who their mysterious new enemy might be. They needed a chance to talk it through – in private.

'Who's this?' Zoe added, her head turning towards Leo. 'Did I hear fighting?'

'Yeah, we heard it too,' Leo said casually, peering up and down the street as if trying to locate where the sound had come from. Shrugging, he turned back to Zoe and jabbed his thumb at his chest. 'I'm Leo, who are you?'

'Zoe. Pleased to meet you,' she said, unwrapping her arms from around Tim.

'Who's this, dear?' Agatha appeared and stood behind her daughter, a soft smile lighting her face.

'Ma, this is Leo.'

'Welcome, Leo. Welcome back, Tim Baker. Come inside, boys.'

A lump formed in Tim's throat. The last time he was here, Hera had trapped Agatha in a fortress. Zoe's family had been punished for making friends with Tim and for protecting him. But rather than kick him out for being a danger to them, they were welcoming him with open arms.

'Thanks,' he said, unwilling to reject her hospitality. 'We won't stay long.'

'Nonsense. Hercules will be home soon. Stay for a meal.' Agatha turned and started walking through the courtyard to the house.

'Cool,' Leo murmured. He pushed his way past Tim and followed her.

'This is a nice surprise—' Zoe started to say, but Tim interrupted her.

'Tell me more about the guy who turned you and your mum to stone. What did he look like?'

After Hera had released Agatha from her fortress, she and Zoe had been attacked on their way home. Tim thought that Hera had set Euryale the gorgon on them. Zoe, however, had been adamant that it wasn't the gorgon. Gorgons were female. They had been attacked by a male.

'He was dressed like a hoplite, but all in black. And he had this really fierce look on his face.'

A shiver of recognition travelled down Tim's spine.

'But the weirdest thing of all was—'

'His helmet plume was made of fire,' Tim finished the sentence for her.

'How did you know?'

'I saw him on the fortress wall, watching the battle. He was enjoying it. The killing, the bloodshed …' Tim gulped. 'He must be a god if he can turn people to stone. I didn't know Hephaestus could do that, though.'

Zoe frowned. 'What's Hephaestus got to do with anything?'

'He's the god of fire, right? It makes sense that he's got a flame on his head.'

'No,' Zoe said. 'I've met Hephaestus. He walks with a limp and dresses like a blacksmith. I only caught a glimpse of this guy, he moved so quickly, but I've never seen him before.'

Tim was growing more and more confused. 'But Hera told Hermes to fetch her son if we caused any trouble. She mentioned flames and ashes. It's got to be him.'

'Her son? That doesn't make sense. Unless ...' Zoe's voice trailed off.

'Unless what?'

Zoe's face was pale. 'Later. I need to think this through first. We'd better go inside.'

Tim followed her into the house, burning with curiosity. Leo was sitting cross-legged on a woven rug, his cheeks working double-time as he feasted on plates of fruit, cheese and honey cakes.

'Your friend has a good appetite,' Agatha said approvingly. 'Join him.'

Forcing a polite smile at the word "friend", Tim sat down and picked up a bunch of grapes.

'Tell us all about yourself, Leo,' Agatha said. 'Is this the first time you've travelled with Tim Baker?'

Tim wondered what Leo would tell her. Would he admit to hijacking the vase? Before he could find out, there was a knock at the front door.

'I'll get it.' Agatha turned and walked through the courtyard. 'Children, keep eating,' she called back.

For once, Leo obeyed an instruction. After a few moments Agatha returned, directing an old man into the room. He was bald, with a curly beard, and was dressed in a crisp white chiton and cloak. His face was creased and the eyes that beamed at them were brimming with intelligence. Zoe bounced to her feet.

'Doctor! My legs are better, see?' She danced on the spot to demonstrate.

'So I see,' the old man said. 'Excellent. And how is your toothache?' he asked, turning to Tim.

It was Hippocrates, the best doctor in Greece. Tim had met him on a previous adventure, when he'd fetched the medical man to heal Zoe's broken legs.

'Gone, thanks.'

'Excellent.' Hippocrates rubbed his hands together. 'Now then. I've come to ask you for a favour. You can help too, young man, if you'd be so kind.' He nodded at Leo.

'What do you want us to do?' Zoe asked.

'My knees aren't what they used to be.' The old man rubbed them with gnarled hands. 'I need some herbs that only grow high up on the mountain. I was hoping you might collect them for me.'

Agatha hesitated. 'We'd love to help, but …' she sighed. 'I don't think it's safe for Zoe to leave the house without her father.'

'BUT MA!

I'll be with Tim and his friend! I won't be alone.'

Tim watched nervously as Leo climbed to his feet, brushing cake crumbs from his chin. 'I'll look after her,' he said, looking steadily at Agatha. 'Nobody will touch her while I'm around.'

Tim narrowed his eyes. Was Leo trying to steal his friends by acting nice?

'It's important, Agatha,' the doctor was saying. 'I have a patient in a bad way. A child touched by madness. She runs raving onto the street, putting herself and others in danger. The only treatment is a potion made of hellebore flowers.'

Agatha looked at Tim and Leo before making up her mind. 'All right. But be as quick as you can. Straight there and back again. No dawdling. And no talking to strange gods.'

'Yes, Ma.' Zoe's eyes shone with delight. 'Don't worry about me, I'll be fine.'

Those words never failed to make Tim nervous.

Clutching Hippocrates' leather pouch, Tim followed Zoe outside. He wished Leo had stayed behind so that he could ask about the man with the fiery helmet. If it wasn't Hephaestus, then who was it?

Instead, Leo was striding after Zoe, eagerly drinking in the scenery.

'Have you and Tim been friends long?' Zoe asked politely, as the tall boy drew level with her. Not wanting to miss what they were saying, Tim hastened to catch up.

Leo grunted non-committally and looked at the path ahead. It wound its way out of the town, towards the looming mountains.

'How come you two dress the same?'
Zoe asked, looking at their school
uniforms.

'The school makes us dress like this,'
Leo said. 'Everyone dresses the same.
Doesn't your school do that?'

'I don't know. I don't go to school.' Zoe
didn't sound happy about it.

'Really?' Leo raised his eyebrows.
'Where I come from, everyone does.
You're so lucky. Wish I didn't have to.'

'Don't you like it?' Zoe was astonished.
'I'd give anything to go, but girls aren't
allowed. We can't do anything fun. We're
supposed to sit inside weaving all day.
BORING!'

'Weaving sounds rotten,' Leo agreed. 'I'd probably skive off and get in trouble.'

'That's exactly what I do.' Zoe smiled warmly at him. 'It's much more fun.'

Leo looked at her in mild surprise, as if recognising a kindred spirit. 'Yeah. Although school could be fun too, I guess. If you had … friends.'

'Don't you?' Zoe looked from Leo to Tim. 'Tim must be a good friend if he brought you to "Ancient Greece", as he calls it.'

'Is that where we are?' Leo stopped in his tracks. 'But time travel's impossible! We just rode a flying vase' – he shook himself – 'which is also impossible. I thought we'd come to another … Well, I thought … Oh I dunno what I thought!'

'Didn't he tell you where he was taking you? That's not very nice, Tim. You should have been more considerate.' Zoe flashed Tim a reproving look.

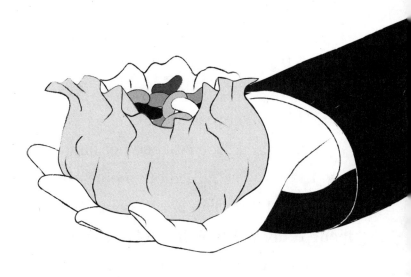

Leo looked pleased at that. 'Have a jelly bean.' He pulled his ever-present bag of sweets out of his pocket and offered it to Zoe.

Tim frowned. As far as he knew, Leo had never offered a sweet to anybody. Ever.

'Ooh, what are they?' Distracted from her questions, Zoe's eyes gleamed. 'Are they seeds? Look at all the colours! What sort of plant do they come from?'

Leo rustled the bag invitingly. 'Try one.' His smile broadened.

Encouraged, Zoe reached her hand into the bag. She pulled out a blue one and turned it over in her fingers. 'This is food? It doesn't look like it.' She shot an apprehensive look at Tim.

'Sure it is.' Demonstrating, Leo popped one in his mouth and chewed. 'See?'

Zoe put the jelly bean in her mouth. 'My gods!' She gasped.

'IT IS SO SWEET!

And so chewy! And so soft – all at the same time! Wow, it's like magic.'

'Try another flavour,' Leo said, thrusting the bag closer. 'Red's the best.'

Tim groaned. Zoe was lively enough. Dosing her up on sweets wasn't wise.

'How come you've never brought me any of these?' Zoe asked Tim reproachfully. 'They're amazing!'

'I prefer your food,' Tim replied.

'Well, I prefer yours!'

The children had reached a fork in the path. One way was broad, gentle and meandering, the other was narrow, steep and rocky. 'Which way do we go?' Tim was relieved to change the subject.

'That way.' Zoe pointed along the steep path.

Tim could see why Hippocrates needed help. Even they would have trouble navigating the rocks and potholes.

'Lucky we've got these to keep us going,' Leo said, offering the bag of sweets to Zoe once more. She eagerly dug out a handful. Leo didn't give any to Tim.

The rest of the walk was accompanied by the sounds of trudging, puffing and chewing. As time passed, the fir trees became sparser and were replaced by stubby bushes. Eventually, they reached a

small clearing. The ground was carpeted
by clusters of pink and purple pansy-like
flowers, their silky blossoms nodding in
the mountain breeze.

Before they set off, the doctor had
described the hellebore plant in detail.
They had to be careful when picking

the blossoms. In large doses, hellebore could be deadly. Taken correctly, though, it could cure madness. Tim wondered whether Leo might benefit from a small dose. Perhaps the shock of time travel had affected his mind, and that was why he was being so nice to Zoe. He might ask the doctor about it later.

'Remember not to rub the petals between your fingers.' Tim reminded them of Hippocrates' advice. 'Snap them off at the stem and drop them in the pouch.'

'Yeah, I know.' Leo left the path and waded through the undergrowth towards the plants. Before he could reach them, however, the air filled with a

harsh cry and a shadow blocked the sun.
Startled, Tim looked up. Hundreds of
strange creatures were wheeling above
them. The swarm was too far away to
see clearly, but one thing was plain: it
was heading straight for them.

The pulsing cloud drew nearer. Near enough for Tim to see that it was a massive flock of birds. His first thought was that Hera's peacocks had found them, but he'd never seen so many before, and he'd certainly never seen them fly. He glanced around nervously. There was no sign of her. Then, as the birds came closer, Tim realised that they didn't look much like peacocks. Their feathers were red and yellow instead of blue, and they had shorter, stubbier tails.

'What are they?' Tim asked, shading his eyes and squinting as shafts of sunlight pierced the swarm.

'OH NO!

They're after the flowers!'

Zoe was right. Without a sound, the flock dived at the hellebore blossoms, turning their snapping beaks and beady eyes to the ground. Ripping and shredding, the strange birds started to devour the plants that Hippocrates had asked them to collect. At this rate, there'd be nothing left for his patient.

'Garr!' Leo ran at the birds, flapping

and waving his arms. 'Get outta there!'

Tim and Zoe joined him. Trying not to damage the flowers themselves, they waded in to shoo the birds away. Screeching with annoyance, the flock twisted and rose as one. It soared over them, packed so densely it eclipsed the sun. It was working! The birds were leaving!

Or … maybe not.

The strange red-and-yellow formation spun and dived again. This time they aimed directly at Tim and his friends, but rose at the last moment to shoot over their heads.

'Ow!' Tim cried as something thick and wet scalded his wrist. 'It burns!'

Zoe stared as Tim snatched a leaf to wipe the sloppy mess off with. 'Is that–'

'Gross!' Leo yelped, dodging several similar missiles. Two more found their target and started smoking on his blazer.

Beneath the bird poo, Tim's skin had turned bright red and was starting to blister. He winced. 'At least they didn't *all* need the toilet!'

'Uh, Tim?' Zoe said. Just as Leo yelled,

'TAKE COVER!'

The birds had wheeled about to make another pass, carpet-bombing them with hundreds of droppings. The children ducked and scattered, covering their skin as best they could, but they were soon covered in angry red marks. Zoe, in her sleeveless chiton, fared the worst.

'Maybe their nesting ground is nearby!' Tim yelled, remembering what Larry had told him about Australian magpies and swooping season. 'They won't stop until we leave!'

'We'll see about that!' Leo had taken off his blazer to cover his head, and now began flapping it at the birds. 'Go on! Get lost!' Not wanting to stand by and do nothing, Tim did the same.

'Shoo!'

With each swipe of their blazers, the formation scattered a little more, sending birds flurrying this way and that.

'I think it's working!' Zoe cried.

Tim and Leo stilled. The birds did seem to have stopped attacking.

Suddenly, there was a loud *poing!* Something light landed on Tim's head. It slid to the ground, slicing off one of his curls in the process. It was a yellow feather, shimmering like gold in the grass. The edge looked razor-sharp. A few other feathers lay on the ground, glinting evilly.

'My gods!' Zoe gasped as a feather slid down her arm, drawing a trickle of blood. 'What next?'

They soon found out. To the children's amazement, the birds started bursting into flames in mid-air, raining mounds of ash all around them. Smoke drifted over the few remaining hellebore flowers, making Tim cough.

'Whoa! What are they?' Leo asked, ducking away from a sudden explosion over his head.

Zoe had her hands up to shield her face from the heat. 'They must be phoenixes. That's what they do when they're in danger.'

'What stupid animals!' Leo leered, as one by one they continued to explode like fireworks. 'Oh well – that's good! All we need to do is wait until they finish blowing themselves up. Then we go in and collect more flowers.'

Tim wasn't so sure. He'd heard that when phoenixes died, they rose from their own ashes. They might not have much time before they were under attack again.

'We can't wait,' he urged his friends. 'We've got to pick the flowers now.'

Avoiding the smouldering ashes, Tim, Zoe and Leo picked as many undamaged hellebore blossoms as they could find. The bunch looked disappointingly small inside Hippocrates' leather pouch, but it was the best they could do. Hopefully it would be enough.

Curious, Tim picked up one of the fallen feathers. It was stiff and cold like metal. He jabbed experimentally at a flower. The feather sliced through the stalk like a knife through butter.

'Coooool.' It would make a great souvenir of his travels.

Tim gripped the feather carefully and placed it in the pouch, which he tied around his waist to keep his hands free. 'We'd better get the flowers back to Hippocra—'

Tim's words were cut short by the sight of hundreds of baby birds rising from the ashes.

Bald, bedraggled and ugly, the phoenixes grew rapidly before their eyes. Within seconds, short, dull feathers emerged, which soon grew long, sleek and shiny. Soon the birds' heads began to twitch and their beaks to snap. Then they flapped their wings to test them.

'Let's get out of here!' Tim grabbed Zoe by the wrist.

Tim, Zoe and Leo backed away. The

phoenixes fixed them with beady eyes, but didn't move. As long as the children didn't enter the flower patch, the birds seemed happy to keep their toxic poo to themselves. Tim looked at the red marks on his skin ruefully. With a bit of luck, the doctor would have a soothing balm to ease the burns.

'Let's go see Hippocrates.' Tim stepped onto the path leading them home.

They'd only been walking for a few minutes when Zoe clutched her stomach and groaned. 'Urgh, walk slowly, I feel sick.'

'Too many sweets,' Tim said, glancing at her face. It had turned a delicate shade of green. 'You're only supposed to eat a few.'

'Your friend's fine, and he's had more than me! Look, he's still eating.'

'He's used to it.' Tim decided to ignore the "friend" bit for the time being. He would tell Zoe what had happened when he was sure Leo couldn't hear them. 'We'll tell Hippocrates when we get back. He might have something to make you feel better.'

'Good idea– Oops!' Zoe shot out a hand to steady herself as her foot slipped off a wobbly rock.

Tim turned to help her, then froze.

'What? What's wrong?' Zoe asked,

twisting around to follow his gaze.

'UH OH!'

A peacock had appeared on the path and was approaching Leo from behind. The bird flattened its crest before lashing out, jabbing at his hand with a long, sharp beak. Tim saw the bird tweak a bright green jelly bean from Leo's grip.

'Hey, give it back!' Leo made a failed grab for the peacock's beak. With a cock of its shiny head, the peacock swallowed the sweet whole. Leo's face flushed red. 'Oi! That was mine!'

Strutting out of reach, the peacock circled the boy. Suddenly it darted at him and tugged the half-eaten bag of sweets out of Leo's pocket.

'Hey!' Leo snatched at the bag but the peacock wouldn't let go.

'Leave it alone!' Zoe shouted at Leo.

'Get away!' Tim called.

But Leo ignored them. Digging his heels in, he started a tug-of-war with the determined peacock. The bird flapped its wings furiously but refused

to let go. 'Give them back, stupid bird, or I'll thump ya.'

Tim winced. Although Leo didn't know it, he was asking for serious trouble. Sure enough, a thick golden mist formed beside the struggling figures. It soon faded away, and in its place stood a furious-looking Hera.

'How dare you upset my petal!' she stormed at Leo, using her pet name for her birds.

'Your *what?* Leo gaped at her, then his eyes narrowed. 'Does this overgrown chicken belong to you? Call it off! I want my jelly beans back.'

'I will not.' Hera's voice was icy. 'I demand that you give my petal anything he desires.'

Leo did not let go of the bag. 'What are you?' he snarled. 'Some sort of crazy bird lady?'

Tim heard Zoe's sharp intake of breath. 'Is your friend feeble-minded? How can he talk to Hera like that?'

'He doesn't know who she is,' Tim said. 'I didn't tell him anything about Ancient Greece.'

'Don't you think you should have?'

Tim shook his head miserably. It

wasn't as if he'd invited Leo to come along! Still, maybe he should have said something to alert Leo to the dangers they'd face.

'If you do not hand them over at once—' Hera fumed.

'You'll what?' Leo sneered. 'Oi!' At that moment, the bag of sweets ripped. The bright contents scattered on the rocky path. Dropping the empty packet, the peacock started pecking at the ground.

'Get away, Leo!' Zoe called.

'RUN!'

Again, Leo didn't listen. He was busy scrabbling in the grass, grabbing fistfuls

of jelly beans and stuffing them into his pockets. But Hera's head snapped towards Tim and Zoe.

'Aha! I knew this would have something to do with you, Timothy Baker,' she hissed. 'Always causing trouble. Well, this is the last time!' Eyes flashing, she reached down and plucked Leo up by his collar.

'Hey!' Leo's eyes bulged, as if he couldn't believe that such a delicate-looking woman could hoist him into the air so easily.

'LEAVE HIM ALONE!'

Tim shouted, watching with horror as Leo's legs kicked the air. His face was twisted in fury, but he could not escape the goddess' grip.

'Oh, he will be alone all right. Very alone.' Hera raised her free hand. 'For all eternity.'

With a click of Hera's fingers, Leo vanished.

'What did you do to him?' Tim yelped.
'Bring him back! I promise I'll take him
straight home. He'll never bother you again.'

'I don't think so.' Hera dusted off her
hands as if she had touched something dirty.

'Leo didn't know he was doing anything
wrong,' Tim continued to plead. 'It's my
fault. I should have warned him to leave
your peacocks alone.'

Hera folded her bony arms across her

chest. 'If you want him back, go and get him.'

'Where is he?' Zoe demanded, her voice dripping with suspicion.

The goddess smiled craftily. 'A place perfectly suited for someone of his charms and graces.'

'Where?'

'The Underworld.' Hera picked up her peacock and tucked it under her arm. 'It's the best place for him. And for you,' she added, shooting a sideways glance at Tim. 'Enjoy your journey.' With that, the goddess disappeared in a shower of sparkles.

Tim turned to Zoe. 'So what's this Underworld then? Is it a cave or something? How do we get there? We need to bring Leo back.'

'Tim,' she whispered, her face as white as a sheet. 'It's where people go when they die. There's no coming back.'

Tim felt as if someone had kicked him in the stomach. Did that mean Leo was dead? Not that he would miss the bully, but he certainly didn't deserve this!

'There must be something we can do,' Tim said, running a shaky hand through his hair. 'Hera said "go and get him". He can't be dead.'

Zoe shook her head so vigorously her ringlets slapped her cheeks. 'It's too risky. I know he's your friend and everything–'

'He's not,' Tim interrupted.

'What?'

'He's not my friend. He's my worst enemy. I didn't want to bring him here – he made me. That's why I didn't tell him anything.' Sighing, Tim sat down on a boulder. Zoe sat next to him, her face troubled as Tim told her all about Leo's bullying and snooping.

'Well, that's all right then,' she said
when he'd finished.

Tim looked up. 'What do you mean?'

'Leave him in the Underworld. Why
should you care?'

'I – I can't do that!' Tim was shocked.

'Why not? If he's that mean to you,
then good riddance.' Zoe stood up and
brushed off her chiton.

'But – but it's my fault he got caught!'

'No,' Zoe said firmly, 'it's his fault. Why
should you risk your life for him?'

Tim didn't know how to answer. All he
knew was that it wasn't right. He wouldn't
wish Hera's wrath on anyone, not even his
worst enemy.

He drew himself to his feet. His mind

was made up.

'I can't leave him. Sorry, I just can't.' He looked imploringly at his friend. 'I don't expect you to come with me. Just tell me how I get to the Underworld.'

'The usual way is to die.'

Tim flinched at her matter-of-fact statement. 'If we go back to your place and get the vase–'

'What would we say to my parents? No way they'd let us go.'

'There must be another way …'

'Well, yes and no.'

Tim gazed at her steadily. He was not going to budge until she told him.

'Oh, all right.' Zoe sighed. 'You might be able to catch a lift with Hermes. He's

the messenger god, right? Well it's
also his job to accompany souls to the
Underworld. But you can't trust Hermes –
I keep telling you.'

'Hermes saved my life today. The
vase was dropping out of the sky and he
caught us. He could have let us fall, but he
didn't.'

Zoe shook her head. 'Look, even if you
can trust him, it's still a crazy idea. People
have tried to rescue dead loved ones
before. It never ends well.'

Tim clenched his fists. He had to take
the chance. It was the right thing to do.

He looked up. 'Hermes!' he shouted.
'Can you hear me? I need your help!'
He scanned the endless blue sky for the

flying god. Nothing. Tim placed his hands around his mouth and bellowed,

'HERMES!'

'Keep your hair on,' a voice said in his ear. 'You'll wake the dead.'

Tim jumped. The messenger god was standing next to him. 'There you are. I need you to–'

'Take you to the Underworld,' the god finished for him.

'How did you know?'

Hermes grinned. 'A little birdy told me.'

'Can you do it?' Tim wanted to know.

'Course I can. But are you sure you want to go?' Hermes pulled a face. 'They don't like visitors.'

'I have to. Hera sent Leo there. I have
to bring him back.'

Hermes sucked air through his teeth.
'All right. If you insist.'

'I do.'

'Hold my hand.'

Tim took the god's hand and turned to
his friend. 'Goodbye Zoe. I'll try to come
back, but just in case …'

Zoe grabbed Hermes' other hand. Tim
shook his head. He couldn't ask Zoe to
risk herself like that.

'I'm coming.' Her voice brooked no
argument.

'Oh no you're not. Go home right–

ARGH!'

Before Tim could convince Zoe to let go, Hermes had propelled them into the

sky. 'Hold on tight,' the god warned. 'It's not an easy journey.'

They soared over mountains and valleys, creeks and rivers. Tim had the sense of lopsidedness again, as if Hermes wasn't flying quite straight. It was hard to tell, though, because the landscape changed so quickly. Soon it grew bleaker, and the greenery gave way to dirt and dust.

'Hermes, do you know anything about a guy with a flame on his head?' Tim asked as they flew.

'Hmm, let me see. Black hoplite armour, black helmet, plume of fire? Face like two bulls fighting?'

'That's him!' Tim said eagerly. 'Who is it?'

'Dunno. Never heard of him.'

Tim didn't like being teased. 'Hey!'

'*I* know who it is. I've worked it out.'
Zoe spoke for the first time since taking
off. The wind whipping her ringlets
made it hard to see her face. The dread
in her voice, however, sent chills down
Tim's back.

'How would you kno–' Hermes started,
but Zoe cut him off.

'Hera has two sons. You didn't bring
Hephaestus – you brought Hera's *other* son.'

'And … who is Hera's other son?' Tim
asked tentatively.

'Ares.' Zoe's voice was grim. 'The god
of war.'

'Hera meant for you to call Hephaestus, the god of fire,' Zoe continued, squinting at Hermes. 'Instead you went and fetched the war god, and his influence made everyone fight each other. Why did you do it?'

'It was a mistake, all right? Hera should have given me clearer instructions.' Hermes sounded surly. 'Anyway, we're about to land. Best not to look down.'

Tim couldn't help it. He looked down.

Never before had he seen such a bleak landscape. Directly below his feet lay a rocky, desolate shore. Grey soaring cliffs lined the edges of a churning black river. There were no trees, no birds, no signs of life. The only sound was the surging of water as the dark waves rose and fell.

A cold shudder ran through Tim's body.

'Told you not to look,' Hermes grunted. 'That's the River Styx – the boundary between Earth and the Underworld.'

'Hang on. Why are we landing here? Aren't you taking us all the way in? You owe us that much for freeing Ares!' Zoe was indignant.

'BY MISTAKE!

And even I'm not allowed in there. You'll have to find another way.' Hermes nodded towards a skiff tied to a wooden post. Grey and splintering, the little rowing boat looked centuries old. 'Go in that.'

Tim didn't like the idea. He stared at the decaying boat bobbing violently on the seething river. 'What if it sinks?'

'Take it up with Charon.' Hermes descended farther, until they were hovering close to the ground.

Tim bent his knees to keep his feet off the shore, reluctant to touch down just yet. Something didn't feel right. 'Who's Charon?'

'The ferryman. He takes spirits of the dead across the River Styx.' The god was cold and unsmiling as he stared at Tim. 'Lower your feet.'

Tim had never seen Hermes look so grim before. He looked at Zoe's worried face and his bad feeling grew. 'It looks horrible down there.'

'Then I will drop you on your knees.'

Tim forced himself to straighten his legs. An involuntary tremor ran through his body as his feet touched the ground. He could feel its iciness seep through the soles of his feet and spread up his legs.

Hermes dropped the children's hands like stones. He turned away. 'Charon! Come out! Got some customers for you.'

Tim looked around uneasily. Charon was probably like the Grim Reaper:

a skeleton dressed in a hooded cloak, clutching a scythe to reap people's souls with. Biting his lip, Tim steeled himself for a chilling sight.

The figure that clambered out from between two boulders couldn't have been more different. Round-faced and rosy-cheeked, the man raised a hand in greeting.

"Allo 'allo, live ones this time, eh?'
A big smile lit up the man's clear blue
eyes. 'Much better than my usual
customers. They're dead boring. *Dead*
boring, get it?' The ferryman gave a
hearty chuckle, his big belly quivering.
'They don't say much. Worse still, they
never laugh at my jokes!'

Tim smiled weakly. He could see why.

'I hear you're *dying* to cross the river.
Hah!' Charon shook his head and wiped
away a tear of mirth.

'Sort of. Can you take us?'

'Course I can. It ain't far, as the crow
flies. Mind you, it ain't cheap neither.
Cheep cheep!'

Tim winced. 'We have to pay to get

across?' He dug his fingers into his pockets and felt some coins. 'Do you take pounds?'

'Like pounds of flesh? I should say so! All the time! Hah!'

Zoe rolled her eyes. 'Relatives put money in the deceased's mouth to pay for the trip,' she explained. 'One obol each.'

'*A bull?* I'll need a bigger boat!' The ferryman slapped his thighs and doubled over with laughter.

Scowling, Hermes snatched at the air. Two coins materialised in his palm and he thrust them at the chuckling ferryman.

'Excellent. All aboard! I promise you won't get bored. Bored, aboard – get it?'

'Yes. We get it.' Zoe was clearly getting annoyed.

Tim was irritated too, but it could be worse. Charon could have been cold and creepy, like he'd imagined. Tim stepped gingerly onto the rocking skiff. He threw his arms out to keep his balance as it lurched up and then down.

'Are you going to wait here for us?' Tim asked Hermes as he helped Zoe to board. 'Or will you be able to hear us if we call for you to take us back?'

'Who said I'm taking you back?' Hermes was still standing on the shore.

Zoe's head whipped around as Charon pulled the rope off the post and the waves started to pull them away. 'What did you say?'

'Surely you didn't think I was trying to

help you?' Hermes sneered. 'You cost me a sandal.' He jerked a bare left foot into the air, and Tim saw that one of his winged sandals was missing. That explained the lopsided flight.

'How's that our fault?' Tim asked.

'*Everything* is your fault! My life was simple until you came along.'

'Blame Hera, not us.' Tim felt a flash of indignity. 'She started it all. We just protected ourselves.'

'And blame yourself,' Zoe added hotly. 'Hera punished you because you summoned the wrong son.'

'It was a mistake!' Hermes glared at Zoe. 'And this is yours. Hera said she'd only give my sandal back once you were captured.

Thank you for giving me the perfect opportunity!' With that, Hermes leapt into the air and fluttered crookedly away.

Tim fought to hold down rising panic. How would they get back home without Hermes? They'd have to walk. *Could* they walk all that way? Tim shuddered at the thought of being in the wastelands they'd flown over after nightfall. Maybe they should have risked going to Zoe's to get the vase after all. Maybe, if they left now, they still could …

'Um, I think we'd better get off,' Tim said to Charon. 'Can you take us back to shore, please?'

The ferryman looked at him. For once, he wasn't laughing.

'Sorry, son. I thought you knew. This trip is one-way only.'

❦❦

'One way?' Tim gulped. 'So even if we could find our way home from here, there's no way back here from the Underworld?'

'Exactly,' Zoe said through gritted teeth. 'This is a trap we can't escape.'

Tim looked at the ferryman, hoping for a return of the jolly grin. 'That's not right, is it Mr Charon? You can take us back.'

Charon looked uncomfortable. 'None

of that "Mr" stuff. Call me Chaz. All my friends do.'

Tim couldn't help wondering how many friends the ferryman had. Probably not many, given his job.

'Thanks, Mr– Chaz. We don't belong in the Underworld. We're only here because Hera trapped someone we know.'

'Ah, Hera. She's a wild one. Always out for revenge. You know how many souls I've had to ferry, thanks to her?' Charon shook his head. 'Still, she's not as bad as her boy Ares. Most people end up here cos of him, one way or another.'

'What do you mean?' Tim asked, horrified to think that there was someone worse than Hera.

'Hera's spiteful if people defy her. But Ares … he likes killing for its own sake. Battles, sieges, famine, disease. I've had to ferry too many victims of war.' Charon bowed his head. 'Things quietened down for a bit after all the other gods ganged up and imprisoned him. They hate Ares, too. But now …' The ferryman fell silent.

Gripping the side of the lurching skiff, Tim waited for Charon to go on.

Charon stared grimly into the river's depths. 'Ares has escaped. Someone broke his bonds and now he's back to his old mischief.' The ferryman shrugged. 'Still, not your problem. You kids look after yourselves. Don't worry about anything else.'

Prising one hand off the skiff, Tim tugged imploringly at the ferryman's robes. 'Please take us back to shore and we'll find a way home.'

'Wish I could.' The ferryman smiled feebly. 'If I try to take any passengers back with me, dead or alive, the boat rears up and dumps them in the river. I've tried it once before.' He shook his head. 'It wasn't pretty.'

Tim looked at the seething water and gulped. There was no way anybody could swim through that. 'What do we do?'

'Clever kids like you? I'm sure you'll think of something.'

'We will.' Zoe sounded determined. 'With or without your help.'

'That's the spirit. Hah! *Spirit.*'
Charon's lips twitched upwards in the
beginnings of a smile. 'I'm sure you kids
will be fine.'

Tim wanted to believe that, but he still
felt awful. It was his fault they were here.
Zoe had wanted to leave the bully to his
fate – but no. Tim had to go and be a hero,
didn't he? What was the saying? "Pride
comes before a fall." His face burned with
shame.

'It's not your fault.' Zoe must have
guessed what he was thinking.

Tim shrugged. 'I guess.'

'It's not. Look at me.' Tim looked at his
friend. A determined smile was plastered
across Zoe's face. 'We'll be okay. This

is just another adventure. Maybe the biggest one yet.'

Tim smiled at her gratefully.

'All right, everyone out,' Charon said. They'd bumped against a shingle beach that stretched towards a sheer cliff face. 'Last stop – the Underworld. I hope you're not barking up the wrong tree! Barking, get it? Woof!'

'I don't get it,' Tim and Zoe said in unison.

'Oh …' Charon looked surprised. 'Well, you'll soon find out. Mind how you go.' He waited patiently while the children scrambled out of the skiff and onto the beach. 'Hope to see you again some time.'

Tim blinked.

'I mean, in a very long time,' Charon hastened to explain. 'When you're really old. Cheers!'

The children watched as the ferryman departed. A wave of icy, stale air washed over them, misting their breath. They looked at each other, then turned towards the ornate door that was carved out of the jagged cliff face.

'Now what?' Zoe asked.

Tim squared his shoulders. 'We go in. Not much else we can do.'

'Surely we can't just stroll into the Underworld? Isn't there a guard or something?'

Tim tried to stop his teeth from chattering. 'I don't think many people try to break in.'

There was no doorknob, so Zoe reached out a goosebump-covered arm and pushed. The door creaked open. Taking a deep breath, she walked through. Not allowing himself to think about what they were doing, Tim slipped in after her.

The light was so dim, at first all Tim could see were shadows. Mysterious shapes fluttered past, left and right. Whenever he tried to focus on them, they disappeared. Before Tim knew it, he and Zoe had entered a narrow passage, turned a tight corner and–

'WHOA!'

They were inside a gigantic limestone cavern. It was lit by thousands of flickering torches that seemed to float off the walls. A cathedral-like ceiling soared high above them. Shimmering, ice-covered stalactites dripped downwards, reflecting the light and breaking it up into millions of tiny rainbows. Dark tunnels snaked off in all directions. Tim took a deep breath and almost gagged. Like a morgue, the cold air smelt of death.

'It's beautiful,' Tim said, even as he covered his nose and mouth to block the fetid smell.

Beautiful … and terrible. Part of him wanted to stay there forever, while another part wanted to run away as fast as possible.

He rubbed his arms to warm them, and noticed that his burns no longer stung. Maybe there was no pain in the Underworld.

Zoe opened her mouth to speak, but a loud growl withered the words on her lips.

'What was that?' Tim looked around wildly.

Zoe gripped his arm and pointed. Emerging from the shadows was the largest dog Tim had ever seen. It was as big as a horse! But what made Tim's blood run cold wasn't only the dog's size. It was the fact that it had three heads.

Tim's heart beat faster as the three-headed dog turned. It had seen them! A low growl erupted from each mighty jaw. Eyes glowing red, the beast lowered its heads and ambled towards them. It seemed to be in no hurry, which only made Tim more nervous. It didn't need to rush at them because it knew they couldn't escape. The only way out was back down the narrow corridor and onto the shore of the impassable River Styx.

'Cerberus.' Tim surprised himself by knowing the dog's name.

'What?' Zoe was edging backwards.

'It's Cerberus,' Tim said. 'I remember. Your dad told me about it.'

Tim recalled when he'd first met Hercules. The hero had mistaken an old lady's pet dog for the three-headed hellhound who guarded the Underworld.

'He told me that one bite's enough to kill.' Tim gulped as the dog bared its razor-sharp teeth. 'I thought he caught it?'

'He did,' said Zoe, 'but he had to let it go again. No way would Ma let him keep it as a pet. It eats nearly as much as Dad does.'

'Let's hope it's not hungry now.'

The dog had stopped moving towards them. He seemed content to sit on his haunches and watch. Experimenting, Tim took a step forward. The dog lurched to his feet and growled again. Tim hastily stepped back. The dog settled again. It seemed he wouldn't attack them unless they tried to pass farther into the Underworld.

'What do we do? Go back?'

'And try to cross that river?' Zoe shook her head. 'We have to go forwards.'

Tim looked at Cerberus. 'How?'

'Don't know.'

'Great.'

Tim imagined himself standing there for years to come. Eventually, all the people he loved would grow old and journey to the Underworld. Would he still be there waiting when they arrived?

It was while he was considering this grim fate that he first heard the music. The soft, sad notes rose and fell like a summer breeze at a funeral. Before long, the stalactites picked up the

tune, bouncing the notes back into the
air, where they floated and rippled and
grew louder. Soon the entire cave was
humming.

'What's that?' Tim twisted his head
around. There was no obvious source of
the unearthly music.

'It's someone playing a lyre,' Zoe
whispered. She nudged Tim. 'Look.'

Tim followed her gaze. Cerberus' six
eyelids were growing heavy. His heads
lowered bit by bit until they rested across

its massive paws. With a sigh, the dog closed his eyes. Soon the sound of snoring mingled with the music.

Tim and Zoe raised their eyebrows at each other. 'That's handy,' Tim said.

'Maybe for you,' came a melancholy voice. 'But what kind of musician bores his listeners to sleep?'

A young man emerged from a dark tunnel. His long black

hair drooped gloomily over his face, and his grubby chiton was torn in several places. As he walked his fingers caressed the strings of a harp-shaped lyre, and the music grew even sadder.

'I suppose you want me to keep playing,' he said, frowning from underneath his fringe.

'Yes please,' said Zoe, her eyes on Cerberus. 'You've put him to sleep.'

'I put *everything* to sleep,' the young man moaned. 'Sometimes even people. Or maybe they just pretend so that they can avoid me – I can't tell. It's a real drag. I think it's this lyre. It used to be Apollo's. Someone told me it put his audience to sleep once, so he threw it out.'

Tim doubted it. He couldn't imagine anyone sleeping through one of Apollo's punk concerts. And besides, he didn't feel remotely sleepy.

'I play the panpipes too,' the musician continued, indicating the harmonica-like instrument tucked into his waistband. 'But I prefer the lyre.'

'Who are you?' Tim asked. 'Why are you here? You don't look d–'

'Dead? That's because I'm not.' The young man stopped strumming. 'I'm not making you sleepy, am I? I can go away if you like.'

Cerberus stirred.

'No!' Tim yelped. 'Keep playing, please. It's nice.' He let out a breath when the music resumed and Cerberus quietened again. He smiled at the musician, keen to keep him playing. 'I'm Tim Baker and this is my friend Zoe. And you are?'

'I'm Orpheus, the musician. I don't expect you've heard of me.'

'You play really well,' Zoe said encouragingly.

'It's hard to believe, but I used to only play happy music. I did gigs at weddings, feasts, festivals. I even joined the Argonauts and saved them from the sirens by playing my own, more powerful music. Then, one terrible day …' he let out a shuddering sigh, 'my beautiful wife, Eurydice, was dancing to my music in a field. She stepped on a viper and – and it bit her ...'

Tim was aware of Zoe nodding slowly, like she'd seen where this story was going. Orpheus gave her a wan smile.

'Yes. I came down here to get her back. I begged Hades to give her to me. I played such sweet, sad music for him that he finally gave in.'

Tim recognised the name of the god of the Underworld. He brightened. Maybe Hades wasn't such a bad guy! 'He did? That's all right then.'

'You reckon? He told me I had to walk in front of Eurydice. I wasn't to turn and look at her until we got out of the Underworld.'

'What happened? Did he trick you?'

Tim wouldn't be surprised.

'No.' Orpheus flicked his hair out of his eyes, which blazed with a sudden passion. 'Stupid me, I didn't trust him. I turned around too soon. I saw my lovely wife fade away. She'd been there all along. Now she's gone forever. No second chances.' His hair drooped forwards again.

'Why are you still here, then? Why don't you go home?'

'Without Eurydice? What's the point?'

'Um, freedom?' Tim suggested.

'FREEDOM?'

Orpheus wailed, his music reaching a fever pitch of misery. 'What is freedom without my love? What is life without her beauty?

What is–'

'Sorry, we have to go,' Tim said, stepping around the sleeping Cerberus. He felt bad for the sad young man but didn't know how to help him. 'Thanks for putting the dog to sleep, but we're here to rescue someone too.'

Orpheus jerked his chin at one of the tunnels. 'Go find Hades; he's that way. I wish you better luck than I had.'

'Thanks.' Tim squared his shoulders and marched off down the dark tunnel.

Zoe dashed after Tim and shot him a reproachful look. 'We can't leave him! Poor thing, he's so upset.'

'We can't help him, either. Not if he doesn't want to be helped. After we free

Leo, we'll try to convince him to go home
with us. First–'

Just then a strange keening sound came
from the end of the tunnel.

'∈H–∈∈∈∈∈∈∈!'

Then there was an angry garbling.

'Geh ee owwo eyaaaa!'

Then a heavy sigh – but that was
just Zoe.

'*Now* what?'

Zoe sounded more exasperated than afraid, but Tim still shivered at the muffled grunts and bellows.

'Is this the right tunnel?' Tim asked. He really hoped it wasn't. That way they wouldn't have to go down it and find out what kind of beast was lurking at the end.

'Ow, watch it!' Zoe said, bumping into Tim as he halted in the darkness. 'It must be the right tunnel. Orpheus said so.' The beast gargled again. 'He could be wrong, of course …'

'Do you think that's Hades?' Tim asked.

'Of course not. Hades is a god, not a monster. Let's try another way.'

Tim shook his head. There had been dozens of tunnels snaking off from the room they'd left. One led to the River Styx – who knew where the others led? They could be stuck wandering the corridors of the Underworld forever.

'We might get lost,' Tim said. 'Let's keep going and hope Orpheus is right.'

'What if that thing attacks us?'

'Maybe it's not dangerous. Maybe it's just, err … a tormented soul.'

'That's supposed to make me feel

better?' Zoe snapped.

'At least that can't hurt us, right?' Tim was trying to convince himself as much as Zoe. 'Let's go a little bit farther and see what it is. If it's a monster, we'll run away before we get too close.'

'I guess.' Zoe sounded grudging.

'Stay behind me.' Tim trod carefully on the uneven floor, muscles tensed. He was ready to turn and flee at any moment.

The corridor grew brighter. In the distance, Tim could see splashes of light at regular intervals. As they continued, they saw that the lights were torches attached to recesses in the wall. The hideous sounds came again, this time louder. Tim slowed. The first alcove they

passed was empty. So was the next. But the following one …

'GEH EEE OWWWWW!'

Tim leapt so high he nearly hit his head on the tunnel's low ceiling. Stumbling back, he flailed his arms and knocked Zoe to her knees. She squealed as she fell, then laughed with relief.

The sounds were coming from Leo. Tied and gagged, his eyes flashed with fury. When he saw Tim and Zoe, he strained against his bonds.

Tim pulled the gag from Leo's mouth.

'About time you got here!' Leo shouted.

'What the hell is this place?' His voice echoed in the tunnel.

'Stand still!' Tim reached for the rope that bound Leo to the alcove wall. 'How can I untie you if you keep moving?'

'I'm going to fix you up for this, Cinderella,' Leo said, leaning as far forward as his bonds allowed. 'That vase was a trap. You tricked me into coming here!'

Tim burned with injustice. 'You forced your way here! I'm trying to rescue you, stupid.'

'Oi, who are you calling stupid? I'm gonna–'

Zoe elbowed Tim out of the way. She reached up to Leo and angrily tugged the gag back over his mouth.

'—ics ooo ub!' Leo looked both startled and furious.

'How dare you talk to my friend like that?' Zoe planted her hands on his hips. 'He's risked his life to save you. You should be grateful.'

'Mmpf!' Leo's eyes bulged.

'APOLOGISE!'

Zoe demanded. 'Apologise or we'll leave you here forever. I mean what I say.'

Leo fell silent. His wary gaze darted from Zoe to Tim and then back again.

'Forget it.' Tim murmured, reaching for the ropes. 'He can't help being mean.'

Zoe knocked Tim's hands away. 'Yes, he can. He's not allowed to treat you like that.' Standing on tiptoe, she looked Leo in the eyes. 'Tim is the best friend I've ever had. He's kind, and caring, and lots of fun. He'd do anything to help someone in trouble – even you! Oh, yes, he's told me all about you.'

Tim's cheeks burned, but his heart soared like a balloon.

'Apologise.' Zoe repeated.

Defeated, Leo nodded. His gaze fell. 'O-ee.'

'Humph. That's better.' Zoe indicated to Tim that he should remove the ropes. 'Leave the gag on, though.'

Tim grinned. Not a bad idea. 'Don't worry, I'll remove it in a sec,' he told Leo, who glared at him. 'First the ropes.'

Tim tried to loosen them by hand, but all Leo's struggling had made the ropes even tighter, and the knots impossible to undo.

'We have to cut them,' he said, thinking out loud. 'If only we had a knife.' Then he remembered. 'Hey – we do!'

Tim reached into the leather pouch tied to his waist. Amongst the hellebore flowers they'd collected for Hippocrates, was the sharp feather Tim had picked up. He drew it out. It glinted in the torchlight. Gingerly,

Tim tested the edge. 'Ouch!'

Leo's eyes widened when he saw Tim approaching with the feather. He twisted his body from side to side and grunted.

'Don't worry,' Tim said. 'I won't hurt you. Not if you keep still.'

Leo stood motionless. Tim cut deftly through the ropes, which fell to the ground. Leo pulled off his gag.

'What?' Zoe cupped her ear. 'Did I hear a thank you?'

'Don't push it,' Tim said under his breath. It was okay to tell Leo off when he was all tied up, but not when his beefy arms were free.

'Thanks,' Leo muttered, not making eye contact.

'For what?' Zoe asked pointedly.

'Thanks for rescuing me.' His eyes glanced up at Tim, then down again.

Tim smiled. 'You're welcome.'

Satisfied, Zoe nodded. 'All right. Which way do we go now? End of the tunnel?'

Tim kept his eyes firmly ahead as he led the way. He had no wish to see what might be inside the other alcoves; the odd sigh and moan coming from them was enough to make him walk faster. Leo followed close behind while Zoe brought up the rear. Twisting and turning, the tunnel seemed to go on forever.

Finally, they reached the end.

The tunnel opened into a room that was an odd mix between the earlier, cathedral-like cavern and a Greek temple. Smooth, god-made columns rose to a raw, stalactite-covered ceiling. Jagged stalagmites sprouted between shining marble floor tiles. In the centre was a large, golden throne.

The man sitting on the throne appeared to be asleep. Tim took a tentative step

into the room. Could that be Hades? He didn't look how Tim had imagined him. He wasn't scary or regal or strong. He looked … scruffy. His grey robes were shabby. Unwashed hair drooped around his haggard face. His skin was pale and he looked much too thin.

Tim cleared his throat. 'Excuse me, I'm looking for Hades. We need his help.'

'Join the queue.' The man on the throne spoke without opening his eyes.

'What queue?' Tim looked around warily. He couldn't see anyone. He gulped. Was the room full of ghosts he couldn't see?

'I meant it figuratively. Everyone wants a piece of me.' The man sighed. 'I never

wanted this job, you know. We drew lots:
Zeus got the sky, Poseidon got the sea. I
got stuck with this dump.'

'Does that mean–?' Tim tried again.
It was hard talking to someone's closed
eyelids. 'Are you … Hades?'

'Who else would I be?' The man's eyes
snapped open. His irises were a glowing
blood red, just like Cerberus'.

Recoiling from the unnerving gaze,
Tim bit back a gasp. 'I don't want to
bother you, err … Sir.'

'Then don't.'

'When are we getting out of here?' Leo
grumbled. 'I wanna go home.'

Hades groaned. 'Not him again! That
stupid slug wouldn't stop moaning. He

gave the souls a headache. I had to gag
him to shut him up.'

'OI!

Who are you calling stupid?' Clenching
his fists, Leo took a threatening step
towards the throne.

'Are you mad?' Tim grabbed Leo's
shoulder and held him back. He turned to
Hades imploringly. 'We need to get out.
We don't belong here – we're still alive.
Hera trapped my friend and we came
to get him back.' Tim felt Leo twitch at
the word "friend". He'd said it without
thinking. Great. Leo would be sure to
tease him about it later.

'Yeah yeah, yada yada yada. Tell me

something I don't know.' Hades smothered a huge yawn. 'Hera needs to get over herself.'

'Huh?'

'She wants to rule forever.' The god slumped further down into his throne. 'I can't wait to retire, but she wants to go on and on and on an–'

'Does that mean you'll let us go?' Tim dared to hope.

'You know the deal: walk outta here, don't look back, blah blah.' He flapped his hands as if shooing a fly.

'Thank you!' Tim turned to Zoe, who was standing at the tunnel entrance. 'C'mon, let's go.'

'How do we cross the River Styx?' Zoe asked the god.

'Not my problem.' Hades rubbed his face wearily. 'Now leave, before I gag the lot of you! Oh gods, I feel a migraine coming on.'

Tim and Zoe didn't need to be told twice. They dashed back up the tunnel.

Remembering what Orpheus had said, Tim resisted the urge to look back to see if Leo was following. He was unusually silent. Surely he should be panting, or whining, or eating?

'Which way out?' Tim asked when they entered the giant cavern where Cerberus slept on, snoring softly. One head snorted and another snapped at it sleepily.

Zoe peered at the corridors that snaked

off in all directions. 'That one. I can hear Orpheus playing.'

Sure enough, the sound of music floated towards them. Tim followed the sound and Zoe walked beside him. He hoped Leo would have the sense to keep close and not wander off.

'Remember, don't look back,' a gloomy voice said. Orpheus appeared in the corridor with his lyre, his face glum.

'Is he there?' Tim jabbed his thumb over his shoulder at where he hoped Leo was.

'I won't look,' Orpheus said, keeping his eyes fixed on Tim, 'in case that makes your friend vanish. Don't make my mistake, man. Keep walking. Don't look back until you're all the way out.'

Orpheus turned and led the way down the narrow tunnel. Suddenly, with a twang, the music stopped. Orpheus came to a standstill. 'Rats!'

'What's wrong?' Tim asked, almost bumping into him.

'I snapped a string! Do you know how hard it is to get lyre strings in the Underworld?'

'Never mind.' Tim gave him a gentle

push. 'We'll get you a new one if you come home with us. Just keep going.'

'Tim.' Zoe spoke after only a few more steps. She gripped Tim's shoulder. 'The snoring's stopped …'

It took a moment for the meaning to sink in, and another to hear the scuttling of claws. 'Argh! Run!' Tim cried.

A sound like a labouring steam train echoed off the narrow walls, growing louder by the second. Cerberus was awake, all three heads puffing and growling as he chased them. Suddenly Zoe was no longer next to Tim. He was about to twist around and look for her when he remembered: if he caught a glimpse of Leo, the boy would be trapped in the Underworld forever.

'Zoe!' he panted, looking firmly ahead. 'Are you there?'

'Where else would I be? Keep moving!'

Falling silent, the friends ran as fast as they could, with Tim overtaking Orpheus to the lead. Finally, he arrived at the ornate stone door. 'There's no handle!'

'Try pushing,' Orpheus said.

Tim put his shoulder to the door. 'It's too heavy!'

'I'll do it.' Orpheus pressed past Tim and threw himself against the door. It wouldn't budge.

A dense, cloying smell filled the air and grew stronger.

Dog breath.

Cerberus was close.

'You have to pull!' Zoe shouted, frustration in her voice.

Tim hooked his fingers around one of the door's protruding carvings. They slipped, but he kept trying until he had a firm grip. He tugged and the door swung open.

Despite the blast of icy wind, it was a relief to be outside. They surged onto the shore, taking big lungfuls of fresh air. A hand dropped onto Tim's shoulder.

Leo was standing behind him, panting with exertion. 'Thanks for coming to get me … Tim.'

It was the first time Tim could remember Leo calling him anything other than "Cinderella", but he didn't have time to enjoy it.

'Thank him later!' Zoe cried. 'Shut the door!'

With a mighty

WOOF,

Cerberus burst from the tunnel and stood facing them on the shore.

Cerberus edged closer, growling, forcing the friends towards the water. Tim felt a wave of despair: on one side was the vicious hellhound, with three sets of fangs; on the other was the impassable River Styx.

'I've got an idea!' Leo suddenly squatted and slapped his thighs. 'Good dog! There's a good boy. Come here.'

'Are you nuts?' Tim hissed.

'Probably. But I'm good with animals. Come on, big fella,' he said brightly. 'Wanna play fetch?'

Cerberus paused. All three of his heads titled to the side curiously.

'Quick,' Leo demanded, 'give me something to throw.'

Tim scoured the shore. All he could see were stones and boulders. 'Like what?'

'Anything! Just hurry.'

'Take this.' Without hesitation, Orpheus handed Leo his lyre.

'You can't—' Zoe started to protest, then bit her lip.

Leo held the lyre in both hands. 'Get ready to close the door.'

Tim edged nervously around Cerberus.
He stood just inside the tunnel and
wedged himself against the door.

'FETCH!'

Leo flung the instrument past Tim.
Barking excitedly, Cerberus charged
after it. Tim flinched as the dog's fur
brushed against him. Stepping out of the
tunnel smartly, he closed the door on the
unmistakable crunch of powerful jaws
around the delicate lyre.

'You did it!' Zoe hugged Leo. 'Well done.'

Leo shrugged as if it were nothing, but his freckled cheeks turned red.

'And thank you too, Orpheus. We appreciate your sacrifice.' Zoe released Leo and turned to stare at the seething Styx. 'But how do we get home? We can't swim through that.'

'If only we had the vase,' Tim said.

'I don't think it would carry all of us.' Zoe sounded doubtful.

'Maybe it grants wishes!' Leo said. 'We could wish ourselves out of here.'

'It's a vase, not a magic lamp.' Tim dismissed the idea. 'Anyway, we don't have it, so we've got to find another way home.'

Orpheus' shoulders drooped. 'It's not easy. If I were you, I'd take a sip from the River Lethe and be done with it. It's not far from here.'

'Will it help us get back?' Tim asked, his hopes rising. The river water must be magical!

'Nah.' Orpheus' greasy hair fell across his face. 'It makes you forget your troubles. You won't know who you are, but hey,' he shrugged, 'you also won't care.'

'Then why haven't you drunk from it?' Zoe asked, curious.

'And forget Eurydice? Never.'

'Thanks, but we'll pass.' Tim was firm. 'Charon said he can't take us back, but is there another boat we can use?'

Orpheus shook his head. 'There's only one thing you can try. It might not work, though … It probably won't …'

'What is it?' Tim asked. 'We'll try anything!'

'It's a flying horse. Pegasus.'

'Will he come if you call him?' Zoe asked.

'If I play the right tune. But I'm warning you, he's totally wild.' Orpheus pursed his lips. 'They say that only a great hero can ride him.'

'You're a hero, aren't you?' Zoe demanded. 'Can't you tame Pegasus?'

'I said only a *great* hero. I'm just an ordinary hero. Barely even that. I failed in my quest to get Eurydice, remember?'

144

'You tried and that's what counts.' Tim wanted to reassure the gloomy musician. 'But who is the greatest hero?'

'My father, of course,' Zoe said confidently. 'Or maybe Theseus. Can we call him to come and help?'

Tim wasn't so sure. Theseus cared more about his looks than anything else. Hercules was certainly a great hero, but he'd try to wrestle the flying horse into submission and Tim didn't think that would work. He thought of the other heroes they'd met. Perseus was too old and wouldn't want to leave his garden. Jason? Unless something was made of wood and able to float, the boatbuilder wasn't interested. Odysseus? Tim felt a surge of hope. The warrior was strong and brave – he was also cunning. Odysseus might be the one!

'You can't call anyone.' Orpheus cut across Tim's thoughts. 'This is the River Styx, not the centre of Athens.'

'Can't we use the GGG?' Tim asked. Only gods could use the Greek God Grapevine to notify heroes that help was needed. Maybe they could convince Hades to put out an alert.

'See any grapevines?' Orpheus looked up and down the barren shore. 'Nothing lives here, not even plants.'

'How can you call a horse if you can't call a hero?' Leo asked. He didn't sound hostile, just curious.

Orpheus flicked his hair out of his face. 'Watch.' He pulled the panpipes out of his waistband. He played a piercing tune so shrill that the children had to cover their ears. The music grew higher and higher in pitch, until Tim thought that it had stopped, then realised that he just couldn't hear it anymore. He guessed that it was like a giant dog whistle, emitting a sound that only certain animals could hear.

In a flash of silver light, a gleaming white horse appeared above them. His majestic wings arched as he glided to the ground. He was huge – big enough to carry them all on his back. But would he take them? Pegasus didn't look savage. Entranced by the music, the animal gazed at Orpheus adoringly. As soon as the musician stopped, however–

'Argh!' Zoe shrieked as the horse reared onto his hind legs. He kicked his front hooves at the children and neighed furiously. 'Keep playing!'

Thankfully, Orpheus did. Pegasus stopped thrashing. With a soft whinny, he settled once more, and fixed his liquid brown eyes on the musician.

'We can get on now,' Tim said.

'Dumb idea,' Leo said. 'As soon as the music stops, he'll throw us off. What if we're in mid-air?'

'I wouldn't … risk it,' Orpheus agreed, speaking in the breaths between blows. 'The calming effect … weakens … the farther away … I am.'

Tim looked at Pegasus. He was truly a beautiful horse, far more striking than the ones he'd seen on a school trip. The class had been allowed to feed the animals sugar lumps. Tim had felt nervous getting so close, but they'd been friendly enough – especially after the tasty treat. If only they had some sugar lumps now!

'Leo.' Tim had an idea. 'Come here.'

'Yeah, what?'

'Hold still.' Tim shoved his hand into Leo's pocket.

'Oi! Whatcha doing?' Leo recoiled, but not before Tim managed to pull out a fistful of jelly beans. 'Give em back, they're mine.'

'Here Pegasus,' Tim cooed, holding out the sweets. 'Who's a pretty boy then?'

'It's a horse, not a budgie,' Leo grumbled.

'Let him try,' Orpheus said, putting down his panpipes.

Amazingly, the horse didn't fly into a rage when the music stopped. It laid its ears flat against its head, but that was all.

'Come and have a sweetie,' Tim said. He held a red jelly bean up enticingly.

Lowering its massive head, the horse took the sweet from Tim's fingers. The feel of its squishy lips made Tim shudder, but he held out another sweet. One by one, Pegasus ate all the jelly beans Tim offered.

While he fed the horse with one hand, he stroked his muscular neck with the other. When he ran out of sweets, the horse snickered and rolled his eyes.

'Got any more?' Tim asked Leo.

'Nope. You took them all.'

The horse snorted and shook its head. It didn't look pleased.

'Want some more, fella?' Tim asked the horse. 'I know where we can get you some.'

Pegasus whinnied.

'But we ... um ... need to get on your back. If that's okay.' Tim felt silly talking to a horse, but Pegasus seemed to know what he was saying. It stared at him for a few moments, then lowered itself to the ground. It was letting them on!

'Quick!' Tim didn't want the horse to change its mind. Zoe and Leo scrambled onto the animal's back first. Tim reached out his hand to Orpheus. 'Come with us. We can take you home. We'll get you a new lyre.'

But the gloomy hero shook his head. 'No thanks. I'd rather stay.'

Tim gazed along the cold, desolate shore. 'You can't be happy here!'

Orpheus smiled sadly. 'Don't worry about me. I'm happy being unhappy.'

This didn't make any sense to Tim, but the hero wouldn't budge.

'Hurry up,' Leo said, gripping onto the horse's mane. 'He's getting restless.'

'Go. Shoo!' Orpheus waved them away.

'Are you sure?' Tim looked over his shoulder as he mounted the horse. 'There's still time to change your mind.'

Except there wasn't. As soon as Pegasus felt Tim climb onto his back, he stood and unfurled his great wings. With one powerful beat, they rose up into the air. The children held on tightly as they soared over the River Styx, and away from the Underworld.

14

By tugging gently on the horse's mane and whispering in his ear, Tim was able to guide Pegasus. He followed the burgeoning landscape to get them back into the land of the living. Then, with the help of Leo who had a very good sense of direction, they spotted the mountain where they'd picked the hellebore blossoms.

Tim urged Pegasus to land and the children scrambled off his back.

'This is where you dropped the jelly beans,' Tim said, looking at the ground. They had to find the sweets before Pegasus grew restless.

'That dumb bird ate most of 'em.'

'There's one!' Zoe plunged her hand into a patch of grass and plucked out a bright orange sweet. 'And another.'

Tim fed the jelly beans to the flying horse as Zoe and Leo rummaged for more.

'Sorry, boy, that's all,' Tim said, handing over the last one. He held his breath. Would Pegasus get aggressive now?

The mighty horse lowered his head and Tim flinched. Was he going to charge at them like a bull? The animal stood motionless, and Tim realised that he was inviting him to pat it. Relieved, he stroked the velvety muzzle. Pegasus wasn't wild.

All the horse wanted was kindness and sugar. A bit like Leo, perhaps.

After a few seconds, Pegasus pulled
away. He unfurled his wings and leapt into
the air. Tim shaded his eyes as he watched
the dazzling white animal disappear.

'Have you still got the flowers for
Hippocrates?' Zoe asked.

'Yep.' Tim patted the pouch at his waist,
pulling the raw skin on his wrist as he
did. He winced. Now that they were back
in the land of the living, his burns had
started to sting again.

'Good. We'll drop them off on the
way home. We'd better not hang around,
though. I don't want Dad fussing over
why I was gone so long.'

'Wait a minute,' Leo said, squinting
at Zoe. 'Your dad's Hercules, right? And

Cinder– Tim said he had a hero living in his house. Same guy, right? And that's how all this started?'

'Err, yeah.' It was pointless to deny it now.

'And you've been coming here, having adventures like this since then?'

Tim nodded.

'That's really …' Leo looked thoughtful, '*cool*. And kinda brave.'

Tim gaped. Was Leo being *nice*?

'But you'd better hand over that vase,

CINDERELLA,

or I'll tell everyone your secret!' Leo shouted so suddenly, thrusting his face so close to Tim's, that Tim took several steps back. He should have known better!

But then, Leo winked. 'You're so easy to wind up. Did you know that?'

Only too ready to agree, Zoe joined Leo in gales of laughter.

■ ■ ■

Hippocrates was happy with the hellebore blossoms and assured the children that they'd collected enough. Before they left, the doctor put a balm on the burns caused by the toxic phoenix poo. The balm was soothing, and the red spots faded.

As they approached Zoe's house, the children heard raised voices. They hastened through the courtyard and towards the living area.

'When did this happen?' They could hear Hercules shouting.

'Not long ago,' came a silky reply. 'While you were out enjoying yourself.'

Tim knew that voice! It was Hera.

'I came to you as soon as I found out,' she continued. 'Despite our disagreements, I do not wish the child harm. How could I? I am the goddess of women and marriage. It's my duty to protect families.'

Zoe snorted. 'Some protector!'

Tim flapped a hand at Zoe to be quiet. Pausing to listen, he strained to hear Agatha's soft voice.

'My daughter fell down a well? How could this happen? I've always begged her to be careful!' The anguish in Agatha's voice was clear.

'Sadly, children don't listen,' Hera said.

'I shall go to the Underworld immediately!' Hercules bellowed. 'I shall force Hades to return my child!'

'Good idea. You do that,' Hera purred. 'The sooner the better.'

Tim and Zoe stared at each other. This was yet another plan by Hera to trap Hercules.

'Don't listen to her, Dad!' Zoe hurtled into the house, Tim and Leo at her heels. 'I'm here!'

The look of surprise and anger on Hera's face was almost comical. 'What! How did you get out, you insufferable brats?

Hermes assured me you were safely in the Underworld. I even returned his sandal!'

'I didn't fall down a well,' Zoe said, running to her weeping mother. 'Hera tried to trap us in the Underworld, but we escaped.'

In a rush, Zoe explained everything that had happened, while Hera glowered at them.

Agatha wrapped her arms around Zoe and Hercules turned towards the goddess. 'You have gone too far this time! Being queen goddess won't save you now.'

'You dare speak to me thus?' Hera snarled. 'I will toss you to my son Ares. He has been released from his prison, did you know that? Not by my choice, mind you. But if there is one thing I can rely on him to do, it is to *destroy*.'

'No!' Tim dashed to the corner of the room, where his vase was stored. Grappling at it with sweaty palms, he turned to face the others.

'What are you doing?' Zoe asked, startled.

'He's running away!' Hera folded her arms and smirked. 'Timothy Baker is showing his true colours. He's leaving his friends to face my wrath, while he tries to slink away to safety. What a brave little hero!'

'She's wrong, isn't she Tim?' Zoe stared at him, not wanting to believe it. 'You wouldn't leave us.'

Tim stood stiffly. This wasn't going
to be easy, but he couldn't think of
anything else.

'I'm sorry, Zoe,' he said in a cold, hard
voice. 'But Hera's right.'

'Don't you dare leave me behind,' Leo growled, advancing on Tim.

Hera reached out and grabbed Leo by the shirt, lifting him easily into the air. 'Let Timothy Baker go,' she said. 'He may think he's escaping, but he's not safe anywhere – not even in his own world. I can still reach out to take him. And in the meantime, I can amuse myself with hostages.'

Tim kept his face blank. He didn't want anyone to guess what he was up to, but he had no intention of running away. A plan had flashed into his head, but it was very risky. Leo had planted the idea earlier on, when he'd suggested that the vase might grant wishes. Tim had no idea whether his plan would work. He was betting everything on a passing remark, and the ancient words written on the back of the vase.

'Oh vase,' he said, his voice wavering. 'Shrink Hera!'

The goddess froze. 'What did you say?' As she spoke, Hera's voice grew higher in pitch.

Was it working? Tim looked at her closely. She did seem to be a little shorter.

In fact Leo's feet were on the ground
again, even though Hera was still holding
his collar.

'More!' Tim urged the vase. 'Make
her tiny.'

Hera continued to shrink, her shrieks
of anger becoming squeaks of disbelief.
When she was smaller than a barbie doll,
Tim said, 'Enough.' He reached
down and picked her up.

'Nothing personal,' he said,
peering into her tiny, furious
face. 'But I can't let you keep
hurting my friends.' With
that, Tim placed Hera gently
inside the magic vase. The
place where she had once

trapped Hercules had become her prison.

'H-h-how?' For once, Zoe was at a loss for words.

Tim grinned. 'I was thinking about what Leo said about the vase granting wishes. Remember what's written on it? "He who holds me commands me."' He shrugged. 'I didn't know if it would work, but I had to try.'

'Tim Baker, you are a genius!' Hercules bounded over to Tim and ruffled his hair. 'I am so proud of you.'

'It was Leo's idea, really.' Tim had to be fair.

'I remember you.'

Narrowing his eyes, Hercules turned towards Leo. 'You're the one who made my friend unhappy. I blew you over like a leaf. Tim Baker, shall I chain this wretched boy to a cliff?'

'NO!'

Tim yelped. 'It's okay. He's a friend now.' The word still didn't feel quite right, but he couldn't think of a better way to pacify Hercules.

'Really? If you say so.' Hercules said.

Leo's face flushed red. He clenched his fists and thrust out his jaw.

'We'd better go now,' Tim said, jumping in before Leo could pick a fight. 'Um … what do we do with Hera? Do you have a jar or something to keep her in?'

'She has to stay in that vase or the spell will automatically reverse, just like when you escaped from the flask.' Agatha laid a gentle hand on Tim's shoulder. 'You'll have to take her home with you.'

'But I can't! Mum's selling the vase. She can't sell it with a miniature goddess trapped inside!'

Agatha didn't look worried. 'I've been thinking about that. Hermes once gave us a replica vase, the fake one he used to trick my husband. We still have it.'

'Oh.' Tim shifted from one foot to the other.

He'd always felt bad for letting Hermes

trick his friend so that Tim could keep time travelling. Hercules had never mentioned the existence of two vases, so neither had Tim. He'd kind of hoped the hero hadn't noticed.

Flushing, Tim stole a look at Hercules.

'Yes, we knew,' the hero said gruffly. 'Right from the start. But I felt bad about banishing you, so I didn't want to say anything.'

Tim felt a ripple of relief travel through him.

'The replica isn't magical,' Agatha continued, 'but in your day it will still be a valuable antique. Your mother can sell that instead.'

'What?' Tim said, followed by 'Oh' and

'Wow!' as Agatha's meaning sank in. 'So I get to keep the magic one? I can use it to come back?

THAT'S FANTASTIC!'

'You can,' Agatha said. 'As long as we're all very careful. Remember, you'll be bringing Hera back with you.'

Tim paled. He would have to keep guard over Hera!

'Don't be tempted to look at her too often. She'll try to cast a spell on you, forcing you to release her.' Agatha must have read the anxiety on his face, because she added, 'But do not worry, Tim Baker. You will be an excellent guard. After all, you've already proven yourself a great hero.'

'I … What?' Tim must have misheard her.

'You rode Pegasus, didn't you? Only a great hero can do that.'

'Yeah, but …'

'Okay, that's enough.' Leo might be acting friendlier, but he clearly didn't enjoy Tim being praised so highly. 'I gotta get home before Nan notices I'm missing.'

Tim didn't explain that the vase would take them back to a time mere minutes after they'd left. Now that he knew he could return to Ancient Greece, he too found that he wanted to go home.

Agatha's remarks had given him a lot to think about.

■　■　■

A week had passed since Tim's mother sold the vase. Tim had been very careful to make sure she sold the non-magical one. He'd also kept the magical vase with Hera inside it hidden. How could he explain it to his mother if she found it?

For the first two days, he couldn't stop himself looking inside the vase to check that Hera was still there. Only for a few seconds at a time, in case she tried to put a spell on him. Then he came up with an idea.

'Oh vase, make yourself invisible – except for when I call you.'

The vase had promptly vanished. 'Oh vase,' Tim said again, crossing his fingers for luck. 'Show yourself!'

It reappeared.

'Awesome,' Tim breathed. 'Vanish again.'

And it did. After that, out of sight was out of mind, and Tim finally felt safe from Hera's influence.

Which was why he was so shocked when he turned on the television a few

days later. Mum was upstairs working on her book, so Tim had the volume down low. A bold red and white banner stretched across the bottom of the screen as a news flash interrupted his show:

BREAKING NEWS
WESTMINSTER'S CLASSICAL
MAKEOVER
Police baffled by sudden appearance of temples

Tim reached for the remote control and jabbed at the volume button.

'It sounds like an April Fool's joke, but it isn't,' the newsreader was saying. Her face was strained but her voice remained steady. 'The Palace of Westminster is gone.'

The familiar image of the Houses of Parliament appeared on screen. 'According to eyewitnesses, moments ago the world-famous Gothic structure was replaced by what can only be described as a complex of Classical Greek temples. This is not a hoax. I repeat, this is not a hoax. We are working to bring you live images.'

Tim's blood ran cold.

The newsreader's voice continued but Tim had stopped taking in what she was saying. A wobbly image, clearly from someone's shaking smartphone, appeared. It was true. Westminster had changed beyond recognition. It looked like a part of Ancient Greece had plonked itself into the heart of London.

Oh no. It couldn't be …

Could it?

Tim rushed up the stairs to his bedroom and flung open the door. 'Oh vase, show yourself.'

The magic vase appeared in the corner beside his desk. Tim rushed over to it. Hands shaking, he gripped the handles and peered inside.

It was empty.

The goddess had escaped.

Look out for Tim's next ADVENTURE!

HOPELESS HEROES

TIME'S UP TIM!

STELLA TARAKSON

Sweet Cherry

Tim Baker's worst fears had come true. The spiteful goddess Hera had escaped into present day London. As soon as Tim saw the newsflash on TV, he knew she had to be responsible. Who else would – or could – turn the Houses of Parliament into a complex of Ancient Greek temples? Who else would replace Big Ben's tower with a lighthouse? It could only be Hera, queen of the Olympians.

Tim had dashed upstairs to check his magic vase, just in case. Maybe he was wrong and the goddess was still trapped inside.

The last time he'd been in Ancient Greece, Tim had used the vase's power to shrink and trap Hera. It only occurred to him because Leo had asked whether the vase granted wishes. Tim had scoffed at first, but he'd been ready to try anything to protect his friends – and it worked!

Written on the vase was the spell, "He who holds me commands me". Tim kicked himself for not realising he could command the vase to do more than just travel through time. He could have saved everybody a lot of trouble if he had.

A few days ago, Tim had commanded the vase to make itself invisible. He hadn't wanted his mum to accidentally stumble across it. He'd also been warned not to look at Hera too often in case she put a spell on him, forcing him to release her. He'd thought making the vase invisible would put Hera out of sight and out of mind. Clearly it had because there he was, kneeling on the rug in his bedroom, clutching an empty vase.

Hera had escaped.

But how? She hadn't broken her way

out – the vase was still in perfect condition. Could Hermes, the messenger god, have released her? He was Hera's servant, and the only god who could travel freely between the past and the present.

It was possible, but Tim doubted it. Hermes' loyalties had been unclear until last week, when he'd made it obvious that his only concern was himself. The winged god would not think twice about betraying Tim or Hera to protect his own interests. He would only release Hera if there was something in it for him.

But all this wondering was wasting time. One thing was clear: Tim needed help. He'd go see Zoe and tell her what had happened. Together, they would come up with a plan.

Tim ran back down the stairs and into the living room. The TV screen was filled by an image of a news reporter beside a broad marble column.

'You'd be forgiven for thinking I'm standing at the Acropolis,' the reporter said, his face bewildered. 'As hard as it is to believe, until minutes ago this was the Palace of Westminster. And now – well, you can see what it looks like now!'

The camera panned back, showing a soaring ancient temple. Unlike the ruins in Greece, however, this one looked new. Tim stared at the stunned people clustering in front of it. He scanned their faces for Hera's pale white skin and jet-black hair. Nothing.

'Nobody knows what happened,' the reporter said, waving one arm towards the temple. 'The change was instant, like something out of science fiction.'

He shook his head in disbelief, then

pressed his finger to the tiny speaker in his ear. 'More breaking news … It appears that hundreds of Ancient Greek statues are popping up all around London. They're causing traffic chaos at Piccadilly Circus and the Strand. Some have appeared on the Underground, leading to a suspension of services on several lines.'

Tim had heard enough. He switched off the TV and ran to his mother's room, where she was busy working on her book. 'Mum, I'm going to a friend's house. Is that okay?'

'Okay sweetheart,' her voice came through her partly open door. 'Make sure you're back for dinner.'

'I will,' Tim said, hoping he could sort Hera out in time. He grabbed the vase. He wasn't lying. He *was* going to a friend's house. 'Oh vase. Take me to Zoe.'

Not wasting a moment, Tim pounded
on Zoe's front door. He heard a patter of
footsteps and then the door was flung open.

'Tim! Good to see you.' Zoe's
welcoming smile faded. 'What's wrong?
You look awful.'

'Hera's-escaped-from-the-vase-and-
she's-running-loose-in-London-changing-
things,' he said all in one breath.

Zoe shook her head. 'What did you say? Slow down and start again.'

Tim took a deep breath and forced himself to speak slower. As he explained, Zoe's dark eyes grew wider.

'Whoa! That's terrible! What are you going to do about it?'

'I – err – I don't know,' Tim confessed. 'I was hoping you'd come and help.'

Zoe's jaw dropped. 'You want me to go to the future with you? Are you serious?'

'Oh, okay. Bad idea.' Tim back-pedalled hastily. Zoe knew nothing of the modern day. The future would be a frightening place for her, full of unknown dangers. It was *his* world that was in trouble, not hers. 'It's too much to ask. That's okay, I understand.'

'Of course I'll come. I've always wanted to see your world.' Zoe clapped her hands with delight.

'LET'S GO!'

'Great!' Tim was happy that Zoe had agreed to help him so readily. 'It might be dangerous,' he felt obliged to say.

'So what?'

'Your dad won't like it …'

'Dad's not here! He's taken Ma to the markets. They'll be gone for hours.' Zoe rubbed her hands together. 'We can go and come back before they even know I'm missing!'

Tim couldn't help feeling relieved. He didn't want to face Hera on his own. 'If you're sure.'

'I'm sure. It's odd, though.' Zoe pulled a face. 'Why's Hera trying to make your world look like ours? Is she homesick or something?'

Tim shook his head. He couldn't believe that Hera was merely in the mood for a spot of redecorating. He suspected a darker motive.

'So, what next?' Zoe continued. 'We track Hera down and trap her in the vase again?'

Tim's arms were starting to ache, and he realised he was still holding the vase. He eased it to the ground. 'No point,' he said, rolling his shoulders. 'She'd only find a way to escape again. We have to think of something else.'

'Can't you ask your guards for help?'

'You mean the police?' Tim shook his head. 'Hera's more than a match for them. Besides, people in my world will think I'm mad if I tell them the truth.'

'That's true. But what could he do about it?'

'He tricked Hera once before,' Zoe recalled. 'He might trick her again.'

'He'd have to do a lot more than that: he'd have to capture her. How's he going to catch a goddess?'

Zoe pursed her lips while she considered it. 'I don't know.'

'There's got to be *someone* who can stand up to Hera,' Tim said.

'Actually, there is one person,' Zoe said. 'I'm not sure we should bother him, though. He doesn't like being disturbed. He's very busy and he shoots thunderbolts at people who annoy him.'

Tim's eyebrows shot to the top of his head. 'Who is it?'

'My grandfather – Dad's dad.' Zoe paused expectantly, as if Tim ought to know who she meant. He came up with a blank and it must have shown on his face.

Zoe rolled her eyes. 'I'm talking about the mighty Zeus – king of the Olympians and god of the sky. Hera's husband.'

Tim nodded. Hera was Zeus' wife but not Hercules' mother, which was why she hated Hercules so much.

✼✼

Tim paused as Zoe's earlier words sank in. 'Um, did you say thunderbolts?'

'Yep.' Zoe nodded.

'Zap, sizzle, fry.

You don't want to get on his bad side.'

Tim gulped. If *Hera* was frightened of Zeus, he must be dreadful indeed. 'Isn't there anyone else?'

'Nope.'

'All right.' Tim didn't like the idea, but what choice did they have? 'I guess we have to try. Where is he? Should we go to his temple?'

Zoe was shaking her head. 'He doesn't like being summoned. It's better if we go directly to his home. Ordinary mortals can't go there, but because he's my grandfather I'm allowed in. You should be all right with me.'

'Should be?' Tim would have preferred something a bit more certain.

'All right, then … *might* be.'

'Otherwise zap, sizzle, fry?'

Zoe shrugged. 'It's possible, I guess. Depends what mood he's in.'

'Where does he live?' Tim asked after a lengthy pause.

'Mount Olympus, of course. We can use your vase to get there.'

Hands sweating nervously, Tim gripped one of the handles while Zoe took the other. 'Oh vase, take us to Mount Olympus.'

In less than a minute, Tim and Zoe were standing in a grand hall. At the centre of the vast space was a giant hearth, surrounded by four soaring columns. Flames shot upwards towards the ceiling, which was covered with bright ceramic tiles. The walls were lined with twelve golden thrones. They were currently empty, a fact for which Tim was grateful. It gave him a moment to put the vase down, catch his breath and think.

'This is the meeting room,' Zoe said. Her voice was low and respectful. 'One throne for each of the Olympians. That's Zeus'.' She pointed at the largest throne. Hundreds of diamonds set in the shape of an eagle glittered on the backrest.

Looking carefully, Tim saw that each throne contained the jewel-studded shape of an animal: a wolf, an owl, a deer, a *peacock*. He could guess whose throne that was. Hera had turned her sacred symbol into something like a guard dog, and Tim and Zoe had been chased by the aggressive birds many times.

'This way,' Zoe said, gesturing. 'Let's hope he's in a good mood.'

'I wouldn't count on that,' said a smooth voice.

Tim snapped his head around. Hermes was walking towards them,

the wings on his cap and sandals pulsing slowly. The messenger god's face was stiff and unsmiling. 'Not after what I've told him about you.'

HOPELESS HEROES

To download Hopeless Heroes

ACTIVITIES
AND
POSTERS

visit:
www.sweetcherrypublishing.com/resources

Sweet Cherry